# Finding You Once Again

## A Novel Written in Verse

### S. H. Miah

MUSLIM FICTION PROJECT

# Contents

# Disclaimer

I ask readers to understand that, in telling any story of mine, a main character may do un-islamic or prohibited things due to their flaws or ignorance. I assure that there is a positive character arc at play in all my stories, and ask of you to remain patient and see it through.

*JazakAllahu Khairan* for reading.

# 1

The wind was harsh,

Unrelenting and unforgiving,

As Tasnim Alam sat on the bench,

Her back arched,

The cold coursing

Over her skin like the arctic

Was ticking over her.

She felt thin,

As the sun in the sky dipped

Behind another layer of clouds.

She felt decrepit,

Thoughts completely wild,

Floating like those clouds,

Except her mind was a hurricane,

With her anxiety the plane


Of an absolute destruction.

The grass beneath her slithered

Over her feet like snakes,


And her heart quaked

As the thoughts attacked her once more.

She was a mother,


And mothers were, most of all,

Supposed to be strong

For their kids,


And for their husbands,

All that depended

Upon them, and mostly them.

But as the grief washed over her,

Tasnim's heart weakened her core.

The chill swept over her with a roar.

# 2

Grief was something Tasnim

Had never ever thought of.

All her grandparents,


On both Mum's side

And her father's side—

They'd all died


Before she could really meet them.

They all died before those pangs

That wracked her now could attack.


And for that,

In a strange twisted way

Tasnim was grateful.

Because had she witnessed

Their deaths too,

It may have broken her spirit


So far that she would've turned

Into a husk of her former self,

Heart filled with unwavering hurt.

# 3

Tasnim had often heard

From her dear close friend Hanna,

That a heart was capable of infinite love.

Hanna read so many romance novels

That her mind was a leaking bucket of cliches.

What Hanna hadn't said, however,

Was that the heart could also feel

The exact opposite, it could feel

Infinite pain, too. Infinite grief that grew

And grew and grew

Until it consumed you.

Consumed everything about you.

And that was Tasnim's feeling,

Like she was sinking,

Despite sitting on a rickety


Bench in an otherwise decent garden,

Into the abyss of her feelings,

Into the void of sorrowful weeping.

# 4

Tasnim stared out at the flowers
That had once grown so vibrant,
That had once sparkled.

Lilies on the downslope
Of the grass patch, white
In their shades of complexion.

Now they turned darker,
As if the grief had gripped
Their stems and petals too.

Next to them was a little pot,
Filled with only a small shoot.
For some reason, unbeknownst,

Tasnim felt the urge to

Kick the thing over

And start anew.


Then the impulse subsided,

And her reality collided

With that grief once more.


The plant in the pot,

Which looked left out to rot,

Was for her son Harun.


He'd been begging her for weeks

To start growing a flower together.

Apparently, they'd done that at school,


And at the year's end,

They had a beautiful flower

Whose petals glistened in the light.

Harun wanted something similar,

So Tasnim picked out

A claret sunflower.


And she'd never seen

Her six year old son

As excited as then.


Tasnim sighed, feeling lower

Than that sunflower's stem,

As if her heart was buried beneath


Layers and layers of soiled grief.

And then a footstep sounded,

Above the howling wind,


And Tasnim turned back

To find her husband Riyad

Holding her son Harun's hand.

# 5

"He wanted to see you," Riyad said.

Tasnim sighed, opened her arms,

And let Harun drop in.


He hugged her tight,

Crying but not really knowing why.

How was Tasnim meant to tell


Her six year old son

That *Nani* would never

Ever see his smile,


At least in this world?

How was she supposed to

Carry his burden and her own?

It all felt so

Jagged, crumpled, pain sharp,

Like Harun's hair whenever gelled


And they had to go to a wedding.

Tasnim and him would play spellings,

And one day they had spelt death.


Harun asked her, as he always did,

What the word meant.

Tasnim didn't have a clue


How she was supposed to tell him.

So she said it was when

People were never seen again.


What she couldn't relay,

At that time anyway,

Was the overwhelming loss and grief.

She glanced up,

Mind now back in the present,

And saw her husband stand.


"What do you want?" she said,

Voice coming harsh and bland,

A strange mixture of


Apathy and too much feeling,

Both combined into a strange sense

Of never ever, ever healing.


Tasnim held onto Harun,

As Riyad walked away,

Perhaps to give her space,


Or maybe to vent his own feelings.

Tasnim hadn't a clue,

But all she really knew

Was that her grief was too true,

To utterly visceral. And that

Harun could, somehow, sense it too.

# 6

Tasnim had no memories of her father.

He'd passed when she was a child.

She remembered a thin beard

That was rough to touch,

That she had often rubbed

With the tips of her baby fingers.

She remembered the scent of honey,

Most likely the sweetness he ate,

Or maybe it was from his personality.

Because she never knew him,

She never felt that pull of grief,

That tug on the heart that felt

All so sickening,

Like her heart was in her stomach,

Churning with everything she ate


In that bubbling stomach acid.

The feeling was rancid,

But of her father she had none of that.


She only had faint memories

Of a wondrous past

She wished would return back.


But regaining the past was impossible,

Was nothing more than a fad.

Life was about progress,


About reaching forward

With both hands,

And grabbing the fate you had.

But that didn't stop the wishing.

Tasnim wished that she had a father,

Someone close like Harun and Riyad,


Because in that moment,

She needed a close confidante

With which to share her grief,


Someone who also felt the pain she had,

Someone who shared the sorrow and

Someone who cried with tears never shed.

# 7

One of the worst parts,

At least in Tasnim's mind,

Was the deluge of people

Who messaged you acting,

Acting like they really cared.

Family members and old friends

All texted and called,

And the conversations were

Awkward at best,

And at worst felt like

Wading through a puddle of mud

To get to the other side.

Sometimes the conversations were suffocating,

Whilst other times they were unrelenting.

One friend banged on for ten minutes,


About how they'd suffered the same thing.

Tasnim couldn't listen, so she slammed the phone down,

And turned back to her quiet contemplating.


Now, another call came,

This time from an unknown number.

Tasnim didn't know whether to pick up,


Or suffer the consequences

In utter silence.

Harun sat beside her now,


Staring at their surroundings.

"Go on, *Baba*, see the flowers,"

Tasnim said to shoo him away.

Luckily, Harun was rarely troublesome,

And complied without question.

He popped off the bench

And began circling the flowers

With a curiosity unmatched

By anything else in the world.

Tasnim then glanced at her phone,

At that unknown number once more.

She sighed, heart quaking,

For a reason she didn't know.

Then, she slid the green button,

And to her ear pressed the call.

# 8

The circling of the wind dimmed

To make way for the air waves

As Tasnim held that call to her ear,


And waited for them to make the first move.

Harun shouted something,

And Tasnim stopped herself from looking over.


*"Assalaamu Alaykum,"* the voice said.

It was a female voice, rough round the edge.

Tasnim replied with her own *salaam*,


Then fell into the silence again.

"How are you, my Tasnim dear?"

Why was this utterly random woman

Speaking as if she knew her?

Speaking as if they were the closest of family?

But Tasnim had lost her closest of kin,


And now that grief came raging

Back to haunt her once again.

"I'm sorry," Tasnim said,


Pressing the bright red button.

She pocketed her phone,

Heart more than spent,


Then glanced at Harun,

And the stormy sky above them.

How much longer could she live like this?

# 9

After the call finished,

Harun swarmed her with a hug,

And then showed something in his fingers.


His nails were brown,

Dirty from digging soil,

But his eyes sparkled with a joy


That Tasnim wished she had,

Wished she could somehow bottle

And drink the whole damn glass.


"I found this, *Amma*. Look."

Tasnim looked, and found a small red petal,

Jutting from his fingers.

She took it in her own,

Felt the soft ridges

Grip the centre of her palm.


The red reminded her of blood,

But she quelled that image

For the lusciousness of the plant.


"Where did you find this?" Tasnim asked.

"In our flower, at the bottom."

But that didn't make sense,


Since petals weren't meant to

Grow before the stem from the shoot.

Tasnim handed the petal back to him,


Then leaned back in her seat.

"You're my special one, Harun," she said,

But all her son did was squirm in her hug.

Tasnim didn't feel like being a parent,

But perhaps that was the only thing

To stave off the grief in her mind—


To be a parent to Harun,

A great Mum, *Amma*,

The same as her own was.

# 10

The worst part by far

Was not the overwhelming grief,

Nor the dozens of griefers

That wished to help

Or state their opinions.

The worst part was dealing

With the death procedures.

Tasnim's husband, in that regard,

Was an absolute angel.

He'd taken charge,

Gotten all the papers,

Called the mosque

To request for a burial.

He'd shut down anyone

Attempting to visit them,


And told them all

To politely bugger off.

He was like a warm bubble


Around her, keeping her safe.

And she couldn't ask for a better place.

But still, she felt this coldness to Riyad,


Like he was the same as the others,

Only trying to help because he had to.

Only trying out of a sense of pity.


But one part Tasnim had to suffer,

Right in the hospital's dungeons,

When they'd shown her mum's body.

# 11

The viewing had been a week before,

Timed as if some art exhibition.

Ruther's Hospital had slapped a time

As if family was merely an artifact,

Nothing more than an old relic now.

Perhaps that was the way society was going,

When they abandoned their parents in old age.

But Tasnim wasn't like that.

She'd visited her mother almost daily,

Since the older woman was still healthy,

Still roaring with life in plenties,

Until her body then gave in.

The hospital smelt of antiseptic,

That tugged her nostrils

And almost pulled them apart.


It smelt pungent like tar,

Alongside the sound

Of a deafening silence.


That silence wrapped over her skin

As if trapping her in,

Pressing against her with the weight


Of carrying her grief and burdens.

The body was on a bed of some kind,

Soft and pale, a sickly white,


As were her mother's dead eyes.

A cloth covered the entire body

Up to the neck, where it ceased,

As if a halted life.

Her mother looked in peace,

Eyes closed and lidded,


Mouth slightly open,

Wrinkles flowing freely

As they were no longer rigid.


The room had been stifling,

With Harun by her side,

Though her son held Riyad's hand


And didn't know what to think.

Harun then said, "*Nani.*"

And that was what broke Tasnim,


Because the hope in Harun's voice

Was the same as that in Tasnim.

And Tasnim couldn't bear to speak

Let alone hear someone else say it.

So she swiftly moved out of that room

And left the entire hospital.


And a week later, whilst sitting in her garden,

She still couldn't fathom a way out of her mess.

And then Riyad came in, came with a proposition.

# 12

The wind calmed a little,

Operating in waves

Like Tasnim's heart did.

The sounds of swaying trees

Didn't cease in the distance,

But at least they quietened.

Harun was still playing,

Kneeling and peering at grass

With an odd satisfaction

One could only have

Whilst in the prongs

Of an innocent childhood.

Tasnim glanced at him

From time to time.

That maternal instinct


Forced her to think of him

Almost every minute of life.

And think of her own mother,


And then the grief,

And then spiral once again.

Footsteps shuffled to her left.


Riyad came in, holding his phone.

"Got a call," he said.

"Got a call...you."


Tasnim sat up,

Slightly alarmed now.

Why would someone call Riyad

When they wanted her?

Tasnim stood, then gripped Riyad's phone.

Could it be the same person—


The one who'd called earlier?

"Are they still on the line?"

Riyad shook his head.


"I spoke to them instead.

But it's quite important.

So we should probably sit."


Tasnim raised an eyebrow,

But sat back down.

Riyad perched next to her,


Which shifted the balance

Of the bench half broken.

But it was their bench,

In the centre of their garden,

And that mattered most of all.

"Riyad, who just called?"


Riyad gave her a look,

And Tasnim knew

It would be another bombshell.


"It was your mother's sister."

But Tasnim's mother, like her,

Was an only child, lonely.


Tasnim almost shot up,

Heart quaking from all sorts,

Mind contorted with impossibilities.

# 13

Tasnim remembered a warm day,

When her mother had taken her

To Southend-on-sea, to the beach.


Tasnim had been ten,

Merely a tween,

Wet behind the ears.


The sun had been glowing

Like a medallion in the sky,

Like Tasnim had won the prize


Of having the best mother alive.

But she had no one else,

No grandparents to call *Nani* or *Nana*,

No one to call brother or sister.

She just had her mother,

And even at that age,


The loneliness was crippling.

She'd swept over the sand

Like a mermaid touching land,


And turned to her mother,

Eyes wide with burning questions,

Questions her mother always answered.


"Why don't we have brothers and sisters?"

Because her mother was an only child, too.

"Because, *shuna*, you are special.


Being alone does not

Mean you have to be weak."

Her mother put an arm over her shoulder,

Pulled her in for a hug

As the sun dipped behind a cloud

And the breeze washed them over.


"Being alone is how the prophets started.

All of them had moments of isolation.

But that didn't mean they were failures."


At that age, the answer had sufficed.

Tasnim walked with her mother,

Sand gripping her toes in a hug,


And she didn't think twice

About the given answer.

But, as she grew older,


She realised the truth.

That, whilst being alone didn't mean failure,

It certainly worsened the hurt.

# 14

"What did she say?" Tasnim asked,

Mind back to her back garden,

With the bench and her husband,


And Harun playing with flowers

In the grassy garden corners.

Riyad glanced at her,


Then averted his gaze, inexplicably.

"The woman said she never knew your mother.

Never knew that she existed.


But the police did.

They had the files from the birthday.

They said—from what she told me anyway—

That her sister has passed away,

And that's when she contacted you."

"But how did she get *your* number?"

@That was what had Tasnim confused.

"That's the strange thing," Riyad said.

"For some reason, your mother knew


Of her own sister, but never told a soul.

Then, she gave the numbers to a friend

She had in the police force.


Your mother, *Amma*, told her

To give the numbers—

Both mine and yours—


To her sister if she died.

And that's how she found us."

None of it made sense to Tasnim.

Her mother had never been one for secrets,

Never been one to hide the truth.

But something was so important here,


Something that she wished to hide.

But for what? Why had she

Robbed Tasnim of an aunt,


Someone that could balance the loneliness

That crippled her pre-marital life?

Tasnim let that confusion brew


Like a stew of questions,

A slew of thoughts in her mind.

But would she, in the end,


Find answers?

She didn't know,

Didn't know a thing,

And then Riyad said,

Turning to her with hair sweeping,

"She wants us to stay with her a week."

# 15

Tasnim and her mother

Never ever kept secrets,

And especially not from each other.


That had been a pact from her childhood.

Her mother and her looped fingers,

All ten of them, every one.


Tasnim's child fingers,

Small and dainty,

Interlaced with her mother's,


And they promised each other,

Under the cherry lights of Tasnim's bedroom,

To be honest with one another always.

But Tasnim, now a mother herself,

Knew how fickle such promises were,

Knew that they couldn't possibly be kept,


Especially not with a protected child.

Some things weren't worth saying,

Not to her own child Harun.


But other things,

Larger things,

Like an entire sibling—


That was almost inexcusable.

And Tasnim thought, for just a second,

What else her mother locked away with her death.

# 16

"Meet in a week?" Tasnim asked,

Then she did a double take.

"Not just meet, but *stay*?"


Riyad, ever the stoic,

Didn't seem fazed,

Held a relaxed face.


"She's your aunt and she wants

To meet the niece she never had.

You might be angry—


Quite understandably—

But it's not her fault, Tas."

Tasnim shook her head,

And for a reason she couldn't grip,

Tears pricked her eyelids,

Threatening to burst through

The self-built dam of emotions.

The air felt stale and hot,

As if singeing her lungs.

Tasnim coughed, then leaned back,

Let the sun prickle her skin,

Let the shivers course her spine

Like they were causing tyre tracks.

"That's not fair," Tasnim said,

And Riyad looked confused.

But Tasnim didn't give him a chance

To speak, to tell her his view.

"I'm never meeting her.

She's lost the plot.

And—how dare she try

To barge into my life?"


Riyad remained calm,

Didn't speak,

Didn't utter a syllable,


And let Tasnim vent her feelings,

Let Tasnim circle the bench.

Tasnim needed somewhere


Where none would find her.

"Come, Harun," she said,

And her son trotted over,


Attached himself by the hand,

And then Tasnim walked him inside.

*I need time to think,*

*Time to get this out.*

But Tasnim, as she stumbled

Through her own house,


Wondered whether the truth,

And nothing but the truth,

Would ever get out.

# 17

There was a part of Tasnim's house

That was filled with memories,

Only positive, not negative.


Riyad, after he'd gotten

A job promotion,

And after Harun's worldly entrance,


Had rented another house,

Right on the outskirts of Ilford.

London was too pricey,


Especially with the crazy housing market

That ballooned like a shooting star

To new heights most couldn't reach.

After they'd moved into this house,

Tasnim felt an affinity

Rush through her at the sight of


The small storeroom on the second floor.

The one under the stairs was what they used,

So the second one remained untouched.


A little basket, from Morocco with its designs,

Was inside, with Harun's toys surrounding it.

Tasnim loved to sit on the basket,


In the relative darkness,

And let Harun play around her.

And she would think,


Mind flitting around thoughts

She could never speak aloud.

She sat there now,

Feet rough against the ground,

Mind stormy with rushing clouds.

Heart running through daggers of doubt.

# 18

After a few hours,

Tasnim finally made her exit.

She sat on the stairs then,


Harun rushing down to the living room.

Her heart pounded her ribs,

And the basis of her life almost slipped.


She didn't know what to think.

Was her mother truly the woman

She claimed to be for so many years?


How many other secrets had she hid?

How many more would be revealed?

What if Tasnim's entire life was a fib?

Tasnim's arms shook against her knees,

So she clasped hands together for strength.

She set her legs on the carpeted stairs,


And watched as Riyad came in.

He'd gotten some time off work for the grief,

And also cooked some meals to help.


Tasnim saw in his eyes that intent again,

But she couldn't let him.

She needed something to do,


So she ran downstairs,

The walls seemingly closing in,

Suffocating her from within


The confines of her own house.

"Let me," she said,

And Riyad's eyebrows knitted.

"Sure," he said,

And Tasnim rushed to the kitchen.

She'd make spinach

And a side serving of beef,

Both beautiful curries,

With jackfruit seeds

In the spinach

For that extra little kick.

She collected the ingredients,

A semblance of hope filling her,

And then the reminder of death,

As it always did, hit her,

Struck her heart.

And her limbs sunk to her sides,

And the enthusiasm was cut,

With grief's sharpest knife

Right to the centre,

The core, of her life.


She began cooking,

Not knowing how to feel,

Not knowing what the future,


In its shades, could bring.

Life was tilting,

For worse and worse.


And Tasnim just hoped,

With all her heart,

That life would manage to turn.

## 19

"I want to go," Tasnim said.

The smell of spinach

Roved the kitchen,


Its scent slightly sweet.

The table cloth was meek,

A deathly white that reeked


Of things that had receded.

Riyad ate the beef,

Forking it and rice


Into his mouth

Whilst Harun sat

With his hands amok with curry.

"Harun, *Baba*, eat properly,"

Tasnim said, but her son was still learning.

Still navigating the new world around him.

"You want to go?" Riyad asked.

Tasnim nodded. "I need to leave,

At least for some time.

I need to get a clear head.

Did she tell you where she lived?"

"In a town,"

Riyad said, "near Cambridge,

With her husband

And a few flowers."

"Does she have any kids?" Tasnim asked.

Riyad nodded. "She told me they all moved out.

Professionals who picked their jobs

Over staying with the family."

Tasnim had friends like that,

So hell bent on making money


And forming a career that any thought of family,

Of a husband and kids,

Fell on their flat and deaf ears.


"A town will be good," Tasnim said.

"I need somewhere to clear my head."

Riyad nodded. "And there's nice restaurants there.


We can get some time off from parenting."

*That would be nice,* Tasnim thought.

*Time to turn back the years almost.*


Harun made smacking sounds,

Fighting a galactic battle

With his rice and beef.

Tasnim paused her eating,

Glanced at Riyad and Harun.

"It's a date, I guess," she said.


And even with all the issues,

She found a semblance of hope,

A lighthouse's faint glow.

# 20

They'd packed their bags,

Gotten the clothes in.

Tasnim still hadn't spoken to her,

Her mother's lost sister.

She didn't want to entertain the idea

Of her mother keeping secrets.

Even though she knew her aunt was real,

The closed-off attitude was a defence mechanism.

But against what was the question.

So, Riyad, Allah bless him,

Did all the difficult talking.

He'd gotten another two weeks off work,

Meaning they'd stay with her for three.

Three whole weeks away from home,

Three weeks in which she'd feel alone.


*Or maybe you'll find something*
*You never thought possible.*
But Tasnim didn't buy her mind's excuses.


The grief was too palpable, too real,

And Tasnim, truthfully, wasn't going for herself.

She was going for Harun, her beloved son.


Tasnim had lost a mother,

But Harun had lost *Nani*.

And if Harun could gain some family,


In the form of Tasnim's aunt,

Then wouldn't that fill the hole?

Tasnim didn't know at all,

But she wouldn't deprive her son

For the sake of her own

Unwillingness to extend the olive branch


And take a chance on someone

She hadn't seen before.

Tasnim now, the day before


They were due to leave,

Walked to her mother's bedroom.

Riyad's parents died long ago,


And since Tasnim only had one left,

Her mother lived with them.

But now that room was empty,


Filled with old dust that floated

As if Tasnim were in a cemetery.

The lights were dead, almost broken,

And the old bed gave off the scent of grief.

The walls were painted a pasty green

That looked, more than alive, rather sickly.


Tasnim closed the door once more,

Steeled her shaking and shaking core,

And prepared herself for what was in store—


A journey to meet family,

For the sake of family,

To find the truth of family.

# 21

Tasnim's mother had always,

Always been fascinated with flowers.

Because they'd lived in the city,

Visions of green were a rarity.

Grass was only in certain spaces,

Unnatural since it was placed.

But her mother wished for nature's embrace

Like she had back in Bangladesh.

Luscious forests and animals roaming,

With a breezy wind

And lots of gardens.

Olive and mango trees,

With not a small number of jackfruits.

Harvests that brought in

A wonderful array to boot.


Tasnim wished her mother was with her,

On the drive towards her aunt's house.

Riyad informed Tasnim that


Her aunt's name was Jolly—

Tasnim suspected it was a nickname,

Since Bengalis were fond of that,


Especially when their real names

Featured more syllables than an instrument.

Tasnim looked out the window


Whilst Riyad drove through the motorway,

And saw bricked buildings turn

To luscious envisionings of nature.

And she wished, once again,

That her mother could be here,

And see her own sister with her,

# 22

The house was scenic,

To say the very least.

Riyad reversed into the driveway,


As both Harun and Tasnim

Craned their necks

To get a better look.


"Look, *Amma*," Harun said,

Pointing out with a stubby finger,

"It's a fountain. I like fountains."


Tasnim did look.

It, indeed, was a fountain,

Streaming water in an endless cycle,

Water that, that morning, glistened.

Water that spoke of hope and life,

Or perhaps Tasnim's grief—endless.


Tasnim lamented once more

How she wished her mother was here,

To experience this whole ordeal with her.


But her mother had kept Jolly a secret,

So that scenario was impossible.

And the dead did not come back to life,


Which Tasnim had gotten through her skull.

"Ready to get out?" Riyad asked,

Glancing in the rear-view mirror.


"We don't have to go, you know.

We can turn right around and head back."

But Tasnim wasn't a coward.

She was someone who fought back

Against the threats of her own mind.

She clenched her jaw, shook her head,


And opened the door

And headed outside.

The sun smacked her scarf,


And she turned to view the house,

Harun with her, beside,

Staring too in wonder.


The house featured white-painted steps

That led to a brown front door,

Imbued with an antique French style.


Glass windows surrounded the front,

Reflecting the beaming sunlight.

A warmth enveloped Tasnim,

Bordering the tentative line

Between oppressive and comfortable.

Tasnim grabbed Harun's hand,


More for her own comfort than his,

And nodded to Riyad.

They grabbed their bags and began walking.

# 23

There were things in life,

Like skydiving,

Where the fear prior

Was so palpable

It could probably be bottled up

And sold to governments

To administer to their prisoners.

Tasnim felt that fear multiple times

All throughout her life.

But there was another fear,

A worse fear,

A fear that was all-encompassing,

A sinking of the heart

That never stopped or ceased.

A grief-ridden fear


Of what the future could bring.

That was the fear Tasnim felt,

Different to that of skydiving.


Because the skydiving fear gave way

To a beautiful airy embrace

As you floated down to the surface.


But Tasnim's fear never gave way.

It was never-ending.

It was here to permanently stay.

# 24

Tasnim held her luggage

Before the front door.

She placed it down,

As the breeze brought in

The scent of death

In the form of fresh air.

"You okay?" Riyad said.

Tasnim jerked a nod,

Not trusting her voice

To translate what was in her head.

Harun bounced up and down,

More than anything excited,

Whilst Tasnim felt this dread

Running right through her veins.

But it was rather tame


Compared to the grief alongside it.

Riyad rang the doorbell

And a chime went off somewhere


Deep within the confines of the house.

Tasnim glanced through the glass window

In the centre of the door,


A circular window wherein blurry shapes,

In an assortment of colours, morphed.

And a grey colour began moving,


Began shifting like Tasnim's fears.

And then the door swung open,

And a man stood there,

A grandfatherly figure

With a smile on his face,

A few teeth missing,


Wrinkles like Harun had

Drawn them all in

Haphazardly and random.


But his brown eyes were warm

As he greeted them.

"Come inside," he said,


After a quick *salaam*.

Riyad turned to Tasnim,

As one final chance


To leave this place

And return to their house.

But Tasnim shook her head,

Filled with that courage.

She grabbed her luggage,

And then walked with son and husband.

# 25

"My name's Aadam,"

The man said,

Leading Tasnim through his home.


"But I am sure you are here

To meet my wife, Jolly."

"That's right, sir," Riyad said,


Ever the polite one

When it came to talking

To those he didn't know.


Tasnim strung her luggage along,

And then Aadam asked to take it,

Since they had prepared rooms.

For some reason she was hesitant

To hand it over, as if

She was losing part of herself.


But that impulse subsided

Into its own stupidity,

And Tasnim passed her luggage on.


The weight leaving her hands

Felt like a weight off her heart,

And she had no clue why.


"Come, let us see Jolly,"

Aadam said, his eyes twinkling,

As if meeting his wife


For the very first time.

The hallways were carpeted

With intricate patterns

And drawings that seemed

To depict ancient Islamic architecture.

Tasnim had once wanted a rug


That featured a similar design.

But an entire house of carpet—

That was like living an optical illusion.


Ornaments and vases

Decorated stands and cupboards

That lined each side,


And Tasnim even spotted,

Through an ajar door,

Some kind of animal hide.


She gulped at that,

Wondering just who her family

Were actually staying with.

A musty scent wafted through the hall,

Too musty for Tasnim's liking,

Like the smell was a thick curry of dust


Being forced through her nose.

She could taste the thickets of dust

As they settled along her tongue.


Harun's hand swiped into Tasnim's,

And she could see fear in her son's eyes.

"What's wrong?" Tasnim asked.


"This house is too big."

Tasnim chuckled slightly.

"You'll get used to it."


Harun wasn't fully convinced,

But he seemed to buy it.

Then a voice rang out,

A voice that stopped Tasnim cold.

"*Assalaamu Alaikum*, Tasnim.

It is me, your Auntie Jolly."

# 26

Tasnim's mother
Had always told her
That first impressions

Were the most important.
That in the first glance
Into someone's eyes

You could tell their inner
Workings of the heart.
You could speak to them

For only a few minutes,
And glean their past.
You could stay with them

For merely a day,

And see whether

They would converge—your paths.


But other people,

Tasnim's mother had said,

Were harder to read.


They hid their true intentions,

Or perhaps were so multi-faceted,

That their faces could not reveal


Their true inner colours.

Tasnim glanced at Aunt Jolly

For the first time in her life,


And immediately knew

That her mother's sister

Was the second type.

# 27

Aunt Jolly had a cheerful face,

With sloped cheeks running down

A few wrinkles that couldn't evade

The moisturiser clearly in place.

She wore a *salwar kameez*

That dripped red and gold down to her shin,

With a wide trouser beneath it,

Covering every inch of skin.

A scarf wrapped over her neck,

And ever since Riyad and Tasnim entered,

That scarf now draped her hair,

Ensuring nothing could be seen.

Her eyes were a sharp brown,

The exact same as Tasnim's mother's.

And it suddenly hit Tasnim,


That the woman she was staring at,

Gleaning her appearance

And her inner self,


Was the sister of her dead mother,

The sister her mother kept hidden

For so many years.


Aunt Jolly's brown eyes twinkled

In almost exactly the same way,

And her hands extended through


The arched kitchen doorway,

To greet Tasnim with a handshake.

But Tasnim couldn't take it,

She couldn't bear the grief

Another reminder of her mother

Would dredge up from the recesses


Of her dwindling heart.

She couldn't take it,

So she ignored Jolly's hand,


Ignored Harun trying to grab

The hem of her abaya,

And Tasnim ran back,


To the stairs,

And rushed up the steps,

Not even knowing where she went.

# 28

Upstairs, the dust was thicker,

And Tasnim's eyes blinded with tears

That created a wet canvas

For her to paint with each blink

And each drip across her cheeks.

She stumbled along the last step

And snapped a hand to the railing,

Saving herself in the nick of time.

Tasnim then climbed

Right to the summit,

And didn't send a glance back down.

She hurled on through the winding hallway,

Ignoring the shouts coming after her.

She was being bad-mannered,

Running through a stranger's house,


But the grief was too strong,

Its pull like a volcano's eruption,

Its grip harder than a boulder's pressure.


Tasnim's feet almost burned

Along the reddened carpet,

That mimicked the colour of blood.


Her heart bled for her mother,

And more tears fell,

And she smelt the foul odour


Sweep through the air

To tinge her nose with dread.

Looking up for a sec,

She found a door

Right at the hallway's end,

Seemingly suspended,


As if a portal created

Precisely for her escape.

She hauled open the door,


Barely looking into the darkness,

And shoved herself inside.

Closing the walls around her tight.

# 29

Tasnim remembered snippets,

Little memories that glistened,

From the childhood she missed.


One such snippet,

As she festered in the darkness,

That came to mind


Was her mother's first plant—

When she had begun gardening,

Turning the backyard into a greenhouse


And causing it to burst

With a splendour,

To young Tasnim's delight.

Tasnim recalled seeing the freesia,

For the first time, and others,

And sensing the array of colours


That shone like stars in the sky.

But after her mother's demise,

Tasnim felt the colour


Drain from her life,

As if the sponge of grief,

Of intense sorrow and regret,


Had sucked out the greens,

Reds, purples, and all their shades.

Taken them out for monotonic


Shades of an infinite grey.

But at least,

In the darkness

Of the room she hid in,

The colour black

Invaded her vision.


It was something different,

Something other than grey,

And Tasnim, within the murk, bathed


Her emotions in it.

She'd lost control,

In a way so embarrassing.


How could the sight of one person

Send her grief over the edge?

How could she be so weak internally


That she couldn't stand to greet

The aunt she hadn't had the chance,

Over her lifetime, to meet?

Tasnim felt meek,

Her hands shaking

As dust penetrated the room's murk.


The room was tiny,

Felt more like a cupboard,

With tools hidden in dark corners,


Like it was an old bike shed.

Tasnim let her eyes rove,

As her heart, with sorrow, bled.


That colour from her life

Had completely disappeared,

And now the newfound darkness


Wasn't faring any better.

Tasnim gripped her abaya

To stop her hands trembling,

And leaned an ear to the door—

Anything to break the silence.

She heard footsteps rising


In volume, growing closer and closer.

And she wondered who it was.

Her husband, Riyad?


Or maybe Harun was the only one

The family would deem

Tasnim as ready to see.


Tasnim listened closely,

Ignoring the musty surroundings,

Ignoring the dusty smell creeping in


To sully her nostrils with a sneeze.

The footsteps were light,

Pressing elegantly against carpet.

It wasn't Riyad, nor Aadam,

Nor Harun since he wouldn't be subtle.

That only left one, the worst, to be the culprit.

# 30

The door rattled a second later,

But not from someone opening it.

Aunt Jolly, who Tasnim assumed

Was on the side of the light,

Knocked on the wood instead,

Shaking it lightly, raining spits of dust.

The crux of the matter was

That Tasnim couldn't take

Seeing her mother's sister,

For the similarities were too much.

"Tasnim, you okay?"

The voice punched through the rust.

Tasnim said not a word,

Kept her mouth shut,

Kept her voice tucked

Into her fear.

"Tasnim, we all want you here.

I want you here, my dear,

So there is nothing to be afraid of."

But that was the problem wasn't it?

Tasnim was more afraid than anything,

And she couldn't bear to see

Anyone who resembled her mother

So closely it was like they were one.

"I have old stories,"

Aunt Jolly said,

And Tasnim's skin froze.

The cupboard grew hot,

Spiking heat down her spine,

And her abaya's stifle did little to help.


"Life stories I can tell you over tea."

Tasnim's mother had never liked tea,

Odd for a traditional Bengali.


Her mother had only loved coffee,

Drinking a cuppa every early morning,

Since she'd needed it for the rest of her day.


Tasnim couldn't stay here forever,

Couldn't fester in a cupboard,

Waiting for death to come to her


Like it had her mother.

Tasnim sighed,

Let the dust rain over her

And then sat up,

Swishing her abaya

As she crawled to the door.


"I'm coming out," she whispered,

An embarrassing admission,

Since she'd gone to hide,


But had been found by the one person

She'd been hiding from in the first place.

She felt a disgrace as she tugged the handle


And let the dregs of light in,

Washing away the cupboard's darkness,

With those infinite shades of greying.

# 31

Aunt Jolly had kept her promise.

Tasnim was in the garden now,

Heart no longer bleeding

With emotions she couldn't process.

The grass was far more luscious

Than Tasnim's garden at home.

More plants dotted the perimeter,

More flowers that blossomed

In the shafts of sunlight

Peeking out from behind the grey clouds.

Tasnim sipped a tea

That was far too sweet,

Or perhaps she had been

Deprived of so much within

That even the merest hint of tea


Could send her taste buds spiralling.

A table, wooden, set into concrete,

Sat in the centre of the greenery.


The chairs were wooden, too,

Though far more comfy

Than something made from leather or nylon.


Tasnim leaned back

To feel some semblance

Of a comfort that eluded her.


All whilst Aunt Jolly

Sucked a sip of her tea

And set the cup down with a thud.

"You have my eyes,"

Aunt Jolly said,

Staring just under Tasnim's forehead.


It didn't seem like Aunt Jolly

Was looking at her eyes,

But perhaps she was one of those


Whose vision didn't follow

Where their eyes looked to look.

Aunt Jolly sipped again.


Thud. Set it down.

"You have my mother's eyes,"

Tasnim said, nursing her own cup.


"I think we both have

A lot more in common

Than we would like to think."

After saying that,

Aunt Jolly grabbed another sip.

Like many Bengalis,


Aunt Jolly had tea attached to her hip

As a coping mechanism

When social situations grew awkward,


As it had done between her and Tasnim.

Tasnim glanced back at the house,

Which from the rear looked impressive.


Aadam was taking Riyad and Harun

On an impromptu tour of the property.

"How did you get the house?" Tasnim asked,


At which Aunt Jolly laughed.

"We have had it for generations,"

Aunt Jolly said, "and from my grandfather

It passed down to us."

Tasnim then gasped,

Because if it was inherited,


That would mean her mother,

Her beloved mother,

Should've owned a part.


But Aunt Jolly mentioned nothing

About that, nothing at all,

And the secret merely passed.


Tasnim had a sneaky feeling

That in the three weeks she would spend here,

Those secrets would characterise all she touched.

# 32

The house had lots of rooms.

The master bedroom,

Which belonged to Aadam and Jolly

Was off to the side of the second floor,

Right at the end, opposite to the side

Tasnim had gone when she'd run into hiding.

Three other bedrooms were on either side,

Dotting the hallway as Tasnim was led inside

The second master bedroom on the right.

The room was spacious

And had been prepared ahead of time.

A chandelier poked down from the ceiling,

As if intruding on their lives.

The bed was a sickly white

With red coverings.


And despite the homely exterior,

Tasnim got the same impression

As she did the rest of the house—


A kind of uneasiness that she couldn't root out,

A kind of awkwardness that pervaded

Almost everything in the house.


Tasnim, now, sat on the duvet,

Whilst her husband wound down for bed

In the en-suite bathroom.


The room resembled that of a hotel,

Though a homeliness did exude.

From what, though, Tasnim couldn't

Put her finger on.

The light flashed off,

From the en-suite,


And Riyad came out,

Wearing a vest that showed

Off the new muscles he'd built


At the gym, from weight training,

For Riyad a new habit.

He'd taken to awkwardly flexing


Whenever in vicinity of a mirror,

And the muscles did tighten,

Cinching like a knot.


Still, Tasnim couldn't deny

The fact that she found it hot.

But now, he merely sat beside her,

Hair slightly mussed with water.

"You don't look all right," he said.

"What's wrong?" he added.


Tasnim sighed,

Looked to the door.

Harun slept in a room to their right,


Planted beside in case he woke at night.

He hadn't wished to sleep,

Hadn't wanted Tasnim to leave,


But then accepted fate

Once she told him a bedtime story

And sleep slowly over him claimed.


"I'm fine," Tasnim said.

Riyad raised an eyebrow,

But he didn't question her.

After her mother's death,

Tasnim was prone to snap,

And Riyad, may Allah bless him,


Kept mostly silent

When another rant brewed

Within Tasnim's heart.


She sighed again,

Emotions splitting apart

Between fury and anxiety,


And of course the perpetual grief.

Tasnim slumped on her back

And attempted to fall into sleep.

# 33

The next two days passed
In a bit of an awkwardness.
Tasnim would skirt around her family,

Languishing in her room
Whilst Harun played with his father,
And Aadam and Aunt Jolly

Sat around without the niece
They'd, for all this time,
Wished to really see.

Tasnim only came down to eat,
And even then sat in a silence
That everyone didn't appreciate.

Tasnim felt her husband's stares

And her son's confusion,

But she did nothing to quell it.


She still stooged

In that God-awful silence,

And wallowed in that grief.


She felt multiple times

Aunt Jolly attempt to start

Some kind of conversation.


That was the reason they came,

After all, wasn't it?

To reunite family with family,


Harun with a grandmother

He never knew he had.

But Tasnim didn't wish for that.

She just wished for her problems to dissolve,

Melt into nothing over these three weeks,

And then she could revert to her previous life,


Without having to sacrifice

The part of her that wished,

More than anything, to grieve.


But Aunt Jolly, it seemed,

Wasn't as much of a coward,

And on the third day she acted.

# 34

Tasnim couldn't bear her room

Any longer, not with how stuffy it seemed.

Someone had it cleaned the day before,


And then the room seemed a little off.

So Tasnim had gone around the house

Looking for another spot.


She'd found a side room

That acted as a conservatory.

Nothing existed in that bare room


Other than a little desk,

And two chairs around it,

And a large window spanning

The eastern side of the room,

From top to bottom,

And the view was mesmerising.


The sun would dip through the sky

And grace Tasnim with a light

That only she could enjoy,


Since none were here except her.

The flowers outside would glisten

And glint in the light,


Streaming in the sun to feed themselves.

More than once, Tasnim caught

Aunt Jolly walking around outside.


She'd been watering the plants,

Face set into a peace that seemed

Almost, in a sense, never ending.

As if she hadn't a worry in life,

As if her existence was free from strife,

As if everything, for her, was easy and right.


Tasnim was sure Aunt Jolly hadn't seen her,

But Tasnim had been wrong.

Because not five minutes after


Aunt Jolly had disappeared

She entered the conservatory

And sat down beside Tasnim.

# 35

"It's a very nice day out,"

Aunt Jolly said,

Feet carefully set against carpet.


Tasnim tried everything she could

Not to shoot up in shock.

She kept deadly still,


Heat sticking her hair to forehead

Using a thin film of sweat.

The sunlight which had once


Been so gracious

Was not prickling her skin,

Shining into her eyes as if blinding.

"It is," Tasnim said.

"Why have you been ignoring us?"

Tasnim didn't have an answer,

And she didn't attempt to create one.

She merely stayed in her seat,

Letting the leather dig into her spine,

Letting the thoughts roar in her mind,

Letting Aunt Jolly's question brew

Like an overcooked stew.

"I feel like a fool," Aunt Jolly said,

And that made Tasnim turn to face her.

"Why so?" Tasnim asked,

Happy to get the attention off herself.

"I feel like a fool because

I was so excited to get you here.

I thought you would have heard about me

At least once, but you didn't.

And now I feel stupid.


I should have visited once,

Maybe tried to ease our way in.

But now I have invited you,


And it seems you do not want

To be here more than anything."

Tasnim didn't know what to say,


Didn't know what to feel.

All this time, in her mind,

She'd been the wronged victim.


But *who* had wronged her

Was the real question.

A question she couldn't answer.

But another detail stuck out to Tasnim.

"Why did you think that we

Knew who you were?

My mother—she never told me,

Not even a little bit."

"That's strange," Aunt Jolly said,

"Because in the letter her police

Friend sent, she said you knew of me,

Just you had never seen me."

Tasnim's blood ran cold,

And her heart froze over.

That meant her mother

Had lied more than she'd thought.

If it wasn't just hiding a sister,

Then what else could she have lied upon?

Tasnim didn't want to ponder

But her mind flung onto that.

"I didn't even know you existed,"


Tasnim slowly said,

And Aunt Jolly jolted at that.

"So why did my sister hide me from you?"


Tasnim shook her head,

Confusion running rampant.

"I guess we'll find out."

# 36

Aunt Jolly left the little conservatory

To get the letters Tasnim's mother

Had given her after death,

All while Tasnim remained

In her seat, confused,

Bewildered more than anything.

Her mother had never been

The type of person to keep secrets.

She'd never been the kind

To alter reality

And lie to her family.

That had never been her,

Not before, not ever.

But now Tasnim's conception

Of everyone around her

Was up to question.

What if her husband

Wasn't who he said he was?

What if Aunt Jolly

Was someone more mysterious?

What if Harun held secrets from his mum?

Everything was shifting

Contorting beyond

Whatever she could imagine.

Tasnim shook her head,

Leaning further into the leather.

She couldn't keep thinking about things,

@Otherwise she'd make herself go mad,

Make her entire life one sick fad.

And Tasnim didn't wish to resort to that.


Harun then rushed in,

And in his hands was a flower—

Just a normal sunflower.


And he handed it to Tasnim.

"This is for you, *Amma*."

The gesture warmed her heart


Melted the frozenness

That had almost tore her apart.

At least Harun—he was real,


He wasn't hiding anything,

Wasn't playing a part

In the play of Tasnim's life.

"Thank you, *Baba*," Tasnim said,

And she rolled the yellow sunflower's stem

Around her fingers. It was soft,


Like the fabric of the carpet

That cradled her feet as she sat.

Harun let her pat his hair


And then ran back out,

To where Aadam and Riyad

Were waiting for him no doubt.


They'd taken a liking to each other,

And Aadam was the doting grandfather.

It seemed, sadly,


That out of the three,

Tasnim was the only one

Not finding the visit freeing.

She leaned her head further,

As if upside down,

As if she could, with a motion,


Turn her life around.

And it would be turned around,

Just in a way she never expected,


Since Aunt Jolly then came in,

And in her hands were papers,

Papers that could spill everything.

# 37

The writing on the paper

Was handwritten, sacred

In a sense since

It was a remnant

Of her mother's handwriting.

But it sparked a little resentment

In Tasnim's heart

Because it could reveal secrets.

Secrets Tasnim didn't know

If she wished to uncover.

In the harsh white natural light

Floating in through the wall-length window,

Aunt Jolly sat beside Tasnim once more,

And between them was a coffee table.

Aunt Jolly placed the papers down,


Then swivelled around to face Tasnim.

"You can have a read," Aunt Jolly said,

Seeming to not want to relive the memories.


Tasnim sighed, birds chirping outside incessantly.

She gripped the letter in tight fingers,

Then began to read her mother's cursive.


The letter was written

In a stoic sense,

As if her mother was emotionless.


It wasn't the sweeping tale

Of sister's reuniting

That Tasnim had imagined.

Her mother merely outlined

That should she die,

Jolly should take her children in.


The letter was old,

Fraying at the seams,

The paper almost dipped in coffee.


Tasnim's mother must have

Anticipated dying for a while,

Since she'd prepared the letter aforetime.


Tasnim wondered why

As her eyes danced down the page,

Searching for the answer.


But the letter merely gave none.

Just a general *dua*

At the end, for Allah to save them,

The section with the contact information

Had been tipexxed multiple times,

Corrected and updated as the years went by.


And then the letter signed off.

Out of the ordinary, nothing.

But Tasnim fingered the signature


Right at the bottom,

Felt the ridged ink on her skin—

Her mother had written with a fountain pen.


"Did you find something?" Aunt Jolly asked.

Tasnim, heart shaken, shook her head.

She left the paper back on the table,


And averted her gaze from her aunt.

"I felt the same way," her aunt said,

"Felt like there was no answers.

But I am willing to find answers.

To work with you on that.

Do you wish to help me?"


Tasnim didn't say anything,

But fanned out her red *salwar*

And wondered why Aunt Jolly


Was extending the olive branch.

"What's in it for you?" Tasnim asked.

"You lost a mother, but I lost a sister.


I may be forgetful,

But I cannot forget her,

Despite being years removed.


I wish to find the truth,

As much as you do.

So Tasnim, tell me what

Your heart desires for you."

Tasnim glanced at Aunt Jolly,

At the face resembling her mother's closely,

At the wrinkles embedded in skin,

At someone who the truth had eluded

For tens of years and years.

Could Tasnim help that woman?

Was that their destiny, aunt and niece

United in their uncovering of truth?

Tasnim certainly hoped that was the case,

So she smiled despite her internal earthquake.

"I'd like that," she said. "Okay."

# 38

When Tasnim had left,

Harun almost attacked her

With hugs upon hugs.

"Look, *Amma*," he said,

Waving his hands around

Once he'd stopped the hug.

"I got a toy.

*Abba* bought it for me

From the gift shop."

The toy in question was

A peculiar looking train,

And when Tasnim looked closer,

She recognised it as a popular

Children's cartoon, though

The name eluded her.


But true was Harun's excitement.

He whizzed the thing around

Like a plane and less a train,


Making noises with his mouth

And looking utterly happy

In a way Tasnim almost envied—


She would've if he wasn't her child.

Riyad came in after Harun,

Glanced at Tasnim with a smile.


"Local place here has lots to do.

You wanna go on a date here?

We can get Aadam and Jolly

To look after Harun,

At least for a little bit."

Tasnim smiled at that,


And nodded at the idea.

"Sounds good," she said,

"I haven't had a rest in forever."


"Tonight?" Riyad said.

Tasnim nodded. "I'd love that."

Riyad gave her a kiss on the cheek,


Then walked past her in search of Harun.

Given the last few days,

Dinner would be in a few hours,


Handing Tasnim time to think,

Time to feel through her feelings

For any signs of answers or clues.

She walked back to her room

And found it empty,

Left the same as the morning.


Tasnim yawned, settled on her bed,

And whipped her phone out.

She texted Hanna that everything was okay,


Since her only childhood friend

Worried a little too much for her well-being.

Hanna texted back immediately—


She had no kids, only a husband,

And worked a little from home.

So she had all the time in the world


For a little bit of gossip.

'Call me?' Hanna texted.

Tasnim replied affirmative.

Tasnim locked the door,

Then rang Hanna's number,

And immediately Hanna answered.

# 39

"You never call enough,"

Were Hanna's immediate words.

Tasnim let out a laugh

Since her friend said the same

Every single time she called.

"I make enough effort," Tasnim said.

"You're just never available."

"Sis, I'm literally sitting at home

Like a mama duck, but with no kids.

Speaking of kids,

How's little Haruny?"

Tasnim rolled her eyes

Since the nickname was the worst

She had ever heard

In her entire life.

"The little one's fine.

He's with his dad now,

So I got a little time."

"That's good," Hanna said,

"Because what I really wanna know,

Sis, is about that house you're in."

Tasnim rolled her eyes again.

"There's nothing to tell," she said,

"It's a nice house in Cambridge,

And we're just staying here."

"Nice house? That's a bloody mansion

From those pictures you sent.

I bet you there's loads of secrets

Lurking under the beds."

"That's what Harun thinks,"


Tasnim said dryly,

But Hanna wasn't done

In her investigation.


"She ever tell you why your mum

Made her take you in?"

Tasnim shook her head,


Then realising Hanna couldn't see that,

She replied saying they didn't know,

But that they were working on it.


"A mystery," Hanna said,

"I like myself a mystery.

Make sure you fill me in,

I can do some investigating.

I watched Sherlock Holmes, you know."

"That means nothing," Tasnim said,


With a laugh that actually felt genuine.

And for the next hour or so,

Tasnim and Hanna talked


As old time friends,

Without the eggshells

On which she walked


Around the rest of her family.

And for an hour, Tasnim laughed,

And, from her grief, felt free.

# 40

Tasnim and Riyad sat

In a restaurant called

*A Little Bit of Everything,*


Situated on the corner

Of a picturesque cobbled road.

One of the many in Cambridge.


Riyad had picked the spot

Whilst they walked through the road.

He was decisive like that,


Whilst Tasnim flipped and flopped

Between two things

Until her mind eventually dropped

And she chose nothing.

Luckily, the stereo played silence

Across the speakers, not music,


Which provided the chatter

Of other couples

As a soothing ambience.


The food—a steak for Riyad,

A salad for Tasnim—

Was just as delicious,


Savoury like Aunt Jolly's home-cooked meal

With a professional varnish.

Tasnim crunched into her lettuce,


Tasted the sweet dressing

Along both her tongue

And the base of her throat.

The taste was all-encompassing.

"You look relaxed," Riyad said,

Handing her a lovely grin.


"I feel relaxed," Tasnim said,

"Because I finally have a purpose here."

"I thought the purpose


Was to reunite with Jolly?"

The question offset Tasnim,

Who hadn't thought of it like that.


On the one hand,

She'd only come here for Harun,

So he could connect with his grandma.


She'd never expected herself

To have to integrate with Aunt Jolly,

And feel jolly whilst living with her.

She'd viewed it as a necessary evil.

"What's your purpose, then?" Riyad asked,

Slicing up a portion of his steak,


The name of which was too complicated

For Tasnim to remember clearly.

"I'm finding the truth of why


Mum decided to give Aunt Jolly

The letter to connect her and me."

Riyad's eyebrow rose, and he said,


"Is there some kind of conspiracy?"

Tasnim shook her head.

"Just the truth, Riyad.


And nothing but the truth."

Riyad smiled, held Tasnim's hand

Above the white tablecloth.

"You'll find the truth," he said,

With such certainty as if he knew the future,

And that filled Tasnim's well of confidence.

# 41

It had been five days

Into their visit

When Tasnim had a brainwave.


Whilst Harun enjoyed himself

With his newfound grandparents,

And the extra time with his dad,


Tasnim spent her time thinking,

Contemplating her next mode of attack

To find the truth for good.


But where she stood

At that point in time

Was at the line of confusion.

Because, though it *was* a mystery,

Tasnim had not a single lead

From which she could investigate.


And then she remembered—

Her mum's police friend.

Aunt Jolly would know more about that.


So on the fifth day,

Whilst Riyad, Aadam, and Harun

All strode off to *jummah*


At the local mosque,

Tasnim met Aunt Jolly

Preparing samosas in the kitchen


For when the men returned.

"Do you have the contact

Of that police friend of my mother's?

The one that gave you the letter?"

Aunt Jolly stood before a steaming pan

With oil and frying samosas inside.


She wiped her hands on a towel

And slowed the gas,

Then turned to Tasnim.


"Yes, for her I do have

A number saved on my phone.

But I have not called back


Since she last phoned me."

"And when was that?"

"The first time only."


Tasnim ruminated Aunt Jolly's words

As the tantalising scent of chicken samosas

Wafted into her nose

And caused her mouth to water.

"Can I have the number?" Tasnim asked.

Aunt Jolly nodded. Grabbed her phone,

And forwarded it to Tasnim's WhatsApp.

Tasnim smiled, nodded,

And patted Aunt Jolly on the back.

But before she could leave,

Aunt Jolly asked her a question.

"I have noticed in the last days,

That you do not pray all the time."

Tasnim felt rooted to the spot—

She knew it would come up at some point,

Especially since Aunt Jolly and Aadam

Were both Muslims far more devout.

"I...don't know why I don't," Tasnim said,

Knowing how stupid the excuse sounded.

But Aunt Jolly didn't press her, thankfully,

She only said one thing.


"Answers come from Allah, ultimately.

So be sure not to neglect Him,

And He will not neglect you."

# 42

The next day,

The Saturday of the first week

Into their stay with Aunt Jolly,


Tasnim rose bright and early,

Donned a grey abaya

And a matching scarf


That wrapped over her skull

With a comfort nothing else,

Not even the softest cushion


From Nigeria,

Could ever replicate.

And then she remembered

Aunt Jolly's words about prayer,

And decided to make up *fajr* salah,

Since she'd overslept yet again.


Afterwards, she made *dua*

That Allah found her the answers,

And that she'd be able to handle them.


Then, checking her phone for the time,

And giving Harun and Riyad kisses,

She left the house and walked the road down.


The streets were cobbled,

Bricks jutting out as if rising to greet her,

And the sun's glow was less


Irritating, despite the summer,

And more warming than anything else.

Tasnim, ten minutes later,

Walked into *Sidepark Cafe*,

A cafe situated next to a green space

Where children of Cambridge


Played and laughed with that innocence,

That childhood innocence,

Which only understood love.


That was why, after all,

So many traumas started off in childhood—

Because babies could only interpret love,


And when that trust is distorted

Through pain and suffering,

The baby couldn't do anything


But form an association

Between love and that suffering.

An association which took

A lifetime of healing

To cure, if at all.

Tasnim sat watching those children,


After ordering a latte to the window seat.

Her chair was comfy,

Made of nylon and some other


Synthetic material

That Tasnim didn't recognise.

Tasnim crossed her arms,


Letting the warmth sift across them.

And then the latte arrived,

The waitress thanking her with a smile,


And the buzzer for the front door

Rang just then.

Tasnim's eyes rose

To see who it was.

And it was her—

Her mother's police friend.

# 43

The police friend looked

A little worse for wear.

Her eyelashes were sharp

Like they were attempting to snare

Secrets within the air,

And clamp them right shut.

Her gaze was equally as sharp,

With a nose sloped

Like ridged mountains.

She sidled into the seat

Opposite Tasnim,

Without any hesitation.

She didn't look at Tasnim,

Instead grabbing her bag,

And putting her phone within.


Her bag was Burberry,

A very expensive brand

That Tasnim could only wish for.


Tasnim chastised herself internally.

The *dunya's* allure was merely temporary,

And she couldn't be fooled from her mission.


"Lovely to meet you," Tasnim said.

"*Wa Alaykum Assalaam*," the woman replied.

Tasnim flinched in surprise.


The woman was a Muslim,

And her skin was as white

As the English flag.

"How are you, sister?" Tasnim asked,

Whilst in the back of her mind,

Those secrets churned.


But she couldn't hurry the conversation,

Had to bide her time,

In case her mother's police friend realised,


How little Tasnim really knew.

How much she was in the dark,

How many secrets her mother had kept.


"I *am* the one that kept the secret,"

The woman swiftly said.

She placed her bag against her chair,


Then leaned forward to speak.

"I kept her letters a secret for her.

And her plans after death, too."

"What's your name?" Tasnim asked,

Staring at the woman's eyes,

Which were a stark blue.


"Shannon," the woman said,

"Though I now go by Aisha,

Since she's a mother of the believers.


And I look up to her a lot."

Tasnim, though she knew the name,

Didn't know much of the history.


There seemed a lot she didn't know, actually.

Tasnim sipped her coffee,

Letting the sweet bitterness mix


In her belly,

Fusing with the nerves

Bubbling her stomach.

Then Tasnim asked the question

That had been brewing in her mind

For the entire time.


"Why did you keep the secret from me?"

Shannon—Aisha—lowered her head,

And her smile absolutely vanished.

# 44

"I can't tell you exactly," Aisha said,

"Because it isn't my secret to tell."

Tasnim was flabbergasted by that,


So much so that she resisted the urge

To grab her coffee and chuck it all over her.

"That makes no sense," Tasnim said,


"My mother—she's dead.

And you're still keeping the secret?

Why? You know I need to know,


And yet you don't care?"

Tasnim's face went red,

Her eyes almost bulging,

Her veins filled with a hotness

Whilst her eyes held tears unshed.

"I can't," Aisha said,


"I'm almost as indebted to your mother—

To Nusra—as you are.

I can't betray her,


Whether she is alive or not.

I can only carry out her wishes."

Tasnim shook her head,


Those tears threatening

To push through and

Fall down to her chin.


But Tasnim clenched her fists

Under the table,

Rested them on her thighs,

And returned to Aisha.

"Can't you at least give me a clue?"

Tasnim asked, more out of


Desperation than anything else.

Getting angry with Aisha

Didn't present the answer.


But if Tasnim could piece together

The clues of the past of her mother,

Then perhaps the truth would reveal itself


Like sand when the tide parted.

Aisha placed her hand on chin,

White skin darkening


As clouds outside covered the sun,

Like light rays were secrets.

"Fine," Aisha said, after some deliberation.

Aisha swept her hand over her face,

As if telling secrets caused her physical pain.

"There is a masjid," Aisha said,


"One with a women's section."

"What's the masjid's name?"

Aisha then paused, gulped,


Glanced over at the counter

Like she wished to order

In order to stall for time.


"And why did you tell

Aunt Jolly I knew her before?"

Aisha answered that quickly.


"I genuinely thought you did.

But I was wrong,

And that I can admit."

"What's the masjid's name?" Tasnim asked again,

Knowing the detail was of great importance.

"Masjid Hud in Cambridge," Aisha said,


"Named after the prophet.

A man of great strength.

The clue is there. And—"


It was like her voice had stopped working,

And Tasnim felt a shiver

Overtake her entire spine.


"What did you want to say?" Tasnim asked.

Aisha gave her a glance,

A glance that revealed fears within.


"If you wish to find the truth," Aisha said,

"Then you need to be strong, like Hud.

That's the main thing."

# 45

Aisha returned home in a daze.

The skies were darker now

As evening approached

Like the tides of the sea.

Ebbing and flowing,

Back and forth,

Mimicking Tasnim's mind

Over her unfortunate predicament.

Her mother held secrets,

Like Tasnim had predicted.

Held secrets she never told her child,

Or her estranged sister,

And that presented a mystery

For Tasnim to solve,

To finally reveal the truth


Her mother wished to keep hidden.

Tasnim walked back into the house,

Shaken more than anything,


Heart rattled from the events.

The once big house

Now felt nothing but stifling,


And relief flooded Tasnim

As Harun jumped down the stairs

And hugged her around the middle.


"I flippin' missed you," Harun said.

Tasnim held him at arm's length,

And stared into his eyes.

"Who taught you that word?" she asked.

Harun looked confused more than anything.

He shrivelled under Tasnim's gaze,


And Tasnim softened her look.

"It's not a good word, Harun," Tasnim said,

"Don't use it anymore, okay?"


Harun gave a nod.

"I watched it on YouTube," he said.

Now Tasnim was the confused one.


She'd always made sure that,

Even when Harun took her

Or Riyad's phone,


He never went on YouTube

Or watched any other

Kinds of videos.

"Stay here, Harun.

*Amma's* missed you too,

But I need to go do something."


Harun nodded and floated

Through the hallway,

Likely in search of treasure


To discover or explore,

Whilst Tasnim climbed

Up to the second floor,


Barged into her bedroom,

And saw Riyad lying there,

Looking too relaxed.


"Did you give him your phone

To go on YouTube?" Tasnim asked.

Riyad looked guilty, eyes sparking

With the emotion,

But he nodded regardless.

He was her husband, after all,

And he'd never lied to her—

Not even once.

"But you're not supposed to,"

Tasnim said. "We discussed this before."

"Listen, Tas...I just need some time—"

"I'm the one with a dead mother,

And I'm the one who stays at home with him,

But *you're* the one that needs time?"

Tasnim spat the words at him,

And wished she could take them back.But the tongue was a powerful thing,

Such that it could break marriages,

Change hearts,

And bring the collapse

Of entire nations.


"I just need some time to think," Riyad said,

"We both know that you've been distant.

I love you, Tas, and that's never gonna change,


But there are some things that need to,

Otherwise that love might be harder to give.

Love isn't something you have, Tas,


It's something you do,

And you haven't been doing

Much of it lately, have you?"


Riyad then walked out of the room,

Leaving Tasnim alone with her thoughts,

Thoughts that only, to her stress, added fuel.

# 46

The next day, Tasnim

Still thought about Riyad's words,

Still thought about love being


Something of giving,

And not something you possessed.

But Tasnim had bigger worries


Looming on the horizon,

Worries over her mother

And her endless well of secrets.


Tasnim quickly searched,

After eating breakfast with Harun,

Google for Masjid Hud.

It was a short bus ride away from

The large home belonging to Aunt Jolly.

Tasnim filled Aunt Jolly in


On what she had uncovered

From her mother's police friend.

"How can she work for the police,"


Aunt Jolly asked,

"When she has to observe her hijab?"

"She's a revert," Tasnim said,


"I think she was a policewoman

When my mother and her first met.

Now, I don't know, and I never bothered asking."


"So this masjid," Aunt Jolly said,

Skirting around the living room sofa

To look at the glass cabinet,

Filled with pictures from the past,

Though none were of Tasnim

And none of her mother.


"It is not far from here," Aunt Jolly said,

"I can come with you if you want.

This mystery intrigues me as much."


Tasnim smiled at that.

"Are you sure?" she asked,

"I don't want to trouble you


Even more. I'm in your house, after all,

And you've already done so much."

"Nonsense," Aunt Jolly said,


"We Muslims treat our guests well,

And I know you would have done

The same as I am doing.

That is, of course,

Without question.

It is an Islamic thing."


Tasnim smiled wider,

Then heard Harun laugh,

And Riyad's baritone voice follow.


"We can check on them after," Aunt Jolly said,

"Your husband is a good father.

Allah has blessed you there."


Tasnim knew Aunt Jolly was right—

That Riyad was a great father,

A great husband,


And one that she was blessed to have.

She could trust him, and Aadam,

To look after Harun,

At least for a little bit.

"Let's head to the masjid," Tasnim said.

Aunt Jolly nodded. They both got ready.

# 47

Masjid Hud sat on the far end

Of an otherwise bustling street.

The masjid was beautiful

From the outside,

With cream painted walls

And a green door that signified

Almost a path to heaven.

Stairs led up to the entrance,

The women's entrance

Located on the masjid's other side.

It was near *Zuhr* time,

With fresh air and the scent of new life,

Accompanying Tasnim and Aunt Jolly inside.

Inside, the mosque had cream walls

Painted as if the clouds themselves


Had been taken from the sky

And smattered across bricks.

It was utterly mesmerising.


As Tasnim and Aunt Jolly walked

Through the hall to

The mosque's women's section,


She spotted cabinets of glass,

Shimmering in the soft glow

Of the overhead lighting.


And in those cabinets was a stone carving.

Tasnim looked closer,

Amongst the thrush of praying women.

And she spotted an engraving in that stone.

Her skin shocked from the surprise.

The stone read: 'The women's space was comprised

By Hajji Salman, May Allah reward him.'

*Have I heard that name before?* Tasnim thought,

Wracking her brains to figure out from where.

Aunt Jolly stopped beside her.

"Is something the matter?" she said.

Tasnim sighed, glanced at her.

"That name, Hajji Salman. I've seen that before,

But I can't remember from where.

It's at the edge of my memory."

"I know what you mean," Aunt Jolly said,

Wrapping her scarf tighter to her head.

She swept past Tasnim to get a closer glimpse.

But other than that message,

Tasnim noticed nothing.

Nothing at all.


The *adhan* for *Zuhr* then went off,

Buzzing around the loudspeakers.

"Are you going to pray?" Aunt Jolly asked.


Tasnim rarely did,

But she realised that Allah—

He was the only One who gave answers.


Tasnim nodded to Aunt Jolly,

And they both stepped inside

The prayer hall with green carpet.


And all throughout,

All Tasnim could think about,

Was the mystery: how much time?

# 48

After the prayer,

Aunt Jolly spotted some friends,

So went to speak with them.


In that time,

Tasnim looked around

To see if anything else


Was hidden in plain sight.

She found other cabinets,

Shelved with Islamic books,


But nothing of note.

The mosque's women's hall,

From the very top

Of its curved roof

To the carpet below,

Held nothing more than


That engraving in stone.

"Let's go," Tasnim said,

Once Aunt Jolly finished speaking.


They walked out together,

Into the blinding heat

Of the summer holiday.


Parents milled about the high street,

Kids in prams and strollers,

Walking with happy faces,


Sunlight reflecting off their irises.

Whilst Tasnim's head was

Proverbially in the sand.

Her tongue felt bland,

Like her taste buds had given up.

"Fancy a coffee?" she asked,

To which Aunt Jolly smiled.

"Latte with extra chocolate,"

Aunt Jolly said.

Tasnim almost blanched.

"You add chocolate to a latte?"

"You should try it one time.

It is actually quite nice."

Tasnim strode into the shop,

Aunt Jolly on her tail.

And even though the mystery deepened,

Tasnim felt that, at least for a minute,

She could forget and enjoy herself.

# 49

Tasnim and Aunt Jolly

Returned home two hours later,

To a house that was empty.


"Where have they gone?"

Tasnim asked first,

Eyes darting through hallways


And up the stairs.

It felt eerie, creepily so.

And Tasnim didn't know what to think.


But Aunt Jolly, it seemed,

Was completely unperturbed.

"You get used to a quiet house,"

She said, walking through

To the back garden.

Tasnim followed,


More than a little worried.

"Ah, there they are,"

Aunt Jolly said,


And Tasnim's heart filled with relief.

She didn't want mystery

To pile on mysteries,


But why was she so worried?

Perhaps her entire psyche

Was becoming some sort of jittery


Mess that was jumbled

More than her mother's history?

For all intents and purposes,

Tasnim was treading the line

Between answers and her sanity.

She followed Aunt Jolly

Into the garden,

Where Aadam and Riyad

Sat together, on a wall ledge,

Like they were father and son,

Watching Harun play in the sun,

With those flowers he loved so much.

Harun was a nature boy,

And coming to Cambridge

Had caused those tendencies

To shine far more than the offerings

Of a city like London.

Tasnim sighed, signalled to Riyad

To follow her inside the house.

Riyad did so, worry lining his features—

Pursed lips, furrowed eyebrows.


"You all right?" he instantly asked.

Tasnim nodded. "I just need—"

"Someone to listen?"


Tasnim smiled, then told Riyad,

Quickly, what had transpired.

Riyad listened carefully


As Tasnim detailed her meeting

With her mother's police friend,

And her escapade to the masjid.


"Did you pray?" Riyad said.

Tasnim gave a nod,

And Riyad smiled so wide

It was as if the heavens

Had lifted their lid on this world.

"I'm so proud," he said,


Giving Tasnim a hug

And not a small whirl.

"I've wanted you to pray


Regularly for so long."

Tasnim was now confused.

"But why didn't you say anything?"


Riyad rubbed his hair,

And Tasnim wished to

Put the strands back into position.


"I don't...after Harun,

You've had such a hard time,

And I didn't want to pressure you.

I knew that, in time,

You would make a start,

Because someone as good


A person as you

Can't go their whole life

Without submitting to Allah."


Tasnim didn't know what to say,

What to feel, what to think,

But that motivation sparked in her heart.


She remembered something her mother,

The light of her heart,

Had told her one day,


When they were sitting together in the park.

Tasnim had been young then,

Perhaps seven or eight,

And her mother made an off-hand comment,

That asking Allah for something,

Was the simplest way to attain it.


And Tasnim made a *dua* now,

In the deep secrecy of her heart,

That Allah provided her with answers.

# 50

That night, whilst Riyad slept,

Soft snores filling the room,

Tasnim crept her phone out

From under her pillow,

And did a google search.

The name Hajji Salman

Reverberated around her head,

Like a catchy tune in an advert.

She typed it in carefully,

As she had read it,

And clicked the search button.

Not many results came up,

And the ones that did were of

Random celebrities Tasnim

Had never heard of,


Actors who starred in Bollywood.

Tasnim skipped past them,

Then added 'Cambridge' to her query.


The darkness seemed to surround her,

As if watching in, checking to see

The truth behind Hajji Salman.


But the internet revealed nothing

But old articles that went nowhere.

Tasnim spent around an hour


Scouring the entire internet

For any shred of info

She could get her hands on—

But it amounted to almost nothing.

Sleepiness tugged at her eyelids,

And she felt her heart vibrate


With the angst of not knowing.

Then she stumbled across on article,

Just as Riyad gave a big snore,


And Tasnim resisted the urge to giggle.

This article header spoke about an old man

Who lived on the east side


Of the city, and the journalist managed

To snag an interview with him.

The news site was now defunct, text gone,


But someone on a forum sent the link.

Tasnim racked her brains.

Wasn't there a way to see

Old versions of a website?

Some kind of internet archive.

Tasnim found it through some digging,


And it was called the Wayback Machine.

She plugged the link in,

Mind soaring in anticipation.


And she managed to get a hit!

She quickly clicked on the article,

And browsed through the text—


No images, since the archive

Didn't save anything but the raw link.

Tasnim read through, eagerness


Fuelling her eyes to drop lower

Until she reached the bottom.

But it seemed this article,

Written by a Yasmin Komila,

Didn't hold the answers.

The article was on a new women's section


In the Hud Masjid,

Built by a generous benefactor,

But other than that nothing.


It felt as if the writer hid something.

It certainly was the same man.

So Tasnim need to find Yasmin,


Make contact with her,

Speak with her frankly,

And find the ultimate truth.

# 51

It was the start of the second week

Of Tasnim's stay in Cambridge,

And the mysteries had only deepened.


After breakfast with Aunt Jolly,

Tasnim sat in the garden,

Watching Harun play and laugh,


Whilst Riyad went with Aadam

To fix the old man's car.

Tasnim sat back, leaned,


One leg crossed over the other,

Which bunched up her *salwar*,

And made her ache with tiredness.

"Did you find anything?" Aunt Jolly asked,

"I would do my own searching

But I am not the best with devices."


Tasnim nodded, though tentative.

"I found an article,

By someone called Yasmin Komila.


She spoke to this Hajji Salman,

But it was fifteen years ago.

And there isn't much else."


Aunt Jolly sighed. "I know a Yasmin,

But I don't think it is the same one.

Her surname is *Kamila*, but she is over fifty,


So it fits the timeline, does it not?"

Tasnim nodded at that.

"Please let her know.

There's something hidden everywhere,

Everywhere I look, and I

Can't keep living not knowing."


"I know how you feel," Aunt Jolly said,

"I never knew of a sister, and now I do

I must search for the truth.


It is a burning need inside me and you."

Tasnim felt the urge for answers tinge her heart,

And she would wait for her aunt to contact Yasmin,


But for now, Harun sidled up to Tasnim,

Gave her a warm hug, and from her child's love,

Tasnim felt her grief lessened, a little.

# 52

Over the next few days,

Tasnim began praying,

Sometimes heading to Masjid Hud,


With her Aunt Jolly,

And entering the women's section

Built by Hajji Salman.


Tasnim would bow to Allah,

And prostrate, and she felt her

Heart soar, and her burdens lighten.


She remembered being told as a child,

Though she couldn't remember exactly who,

That salah didn't benefit Allah,

But only the person who prayed.

And Tasnim felt that now,

Felt that peace enter her heart,


But it was only for a fleeting moment

Which evaporated after that salah.

Because the grief would attack once more,


And threaten to tear her apart,

And she would spiral into those thoughts,

Of questions, confusion, no answers.


Tasnim, on the way back,

Would speak with Aunt Jolly frankly.

They shared all the knowledge they knew


Trying to see if answers could be reached.

But it only made them more confused.

Through speaking about her mother,

Despite the grief that would ensue,

Tasnim explored sides to her

That she never would've thought to do.


Her mother was someone who brooded,

Though Tasnim had never thought of it.

Tasnim always viewed her mother


As the model parent,

Struck by life's tragedies,

And then raising her daughter.


But that didn't mean the past

Didn't plague her mother,

Didn't haunt her.


Her mother was as susceptible

To ruing the past

As much as anyone else,

And Tasnim knew the answers

To her many questions,

Lay in exploring the past.


On the third day of the second week,

She spoke with her friend Hanna,

And relayed the mystery updates.


And relayed her thoughts

About the secrets lying in

Her mother's past,


Though that past was mostly unexplored.

And Hanna had a brainwave.

"Is there something at your home, girl?


Something that's like a secret

Of your mum's. Like a vase

She never let anyone touch."

Tasnim didn't know.She'd gone into her mother's room,

But had never been the one to snoop.


No one deserved someone

Rummaging through their belongings,

Searching for something private.


But her mother was dead now,

And Tasnim would have to dispose of things,

So why not take a look for anything


To help her solve the mystery?

"Thanks, Hanna," Tasnim said.

"Love you sis, bye."


Tasnim then smiled,

Located in the house Riyad,

And had a favour to ask.

# 53

They were drumming along the motorway,

At breakneck speeds, a flurry.

Or perhaps Riyad was driving normally,

And Tasnim perceived it as fast

Because her mind was

Locked into a frenzy.

They'd left Harun with Aunt Jolly.

Riyad hadn't wanted to,

But Tasnim knew that

Bringing her child along

Would be a big mistake.

Harun wouldn't wish to see

His mother rummaging through

The belongings of the grandmother

That had just passed away.


Before they left,

Tasnim made sure to ask

If he was okay staying with them.


Tasnim felt a little guilty,

But Harun's smile was wide

As the space between earth and sun.


He nodded emphatically,

And ran over to Aunt Jolly,

And that placed Tasnim's heart at ease,


At least a little bit. Riyad reluctantly agreed.

The motorway roared into view once more,

Cars defending their lanes,

As Riyad weaved in and out,

His own car screeching

Like it was desperate for answers too.


The engine rumbled beneath,

Shaking Tasnim's body,

Shaking her mind free


From her previous security.

The way Hanna had worded things,

Meant she believed there to be secrets.


Secrets Tasnim would never see coming,

Secrets that could shock her

Into changing her entire life


And everything she knew about it.

"You all right?" Riyad asked,

Ever the caring husband.

Tasnim gulped, nodded,

Put on a face of resoluteness.

"Yeah, now let's just get there."

# 54

Tasnim thought,

When she'd first arrived at Aunt Jolly's place,

That returning home would be

The best feeling in the world,

That she'd be filled with nostalgia,

And appreciation for her home.

But now the place felt Frankenstein-ish,

Like out of a horror movie.

They arrived home shortly after midday,

But that didn't stop the place

From feeling so eerie,

Feeling like something was out of place.

Tasnim's first reaction

Was asking herself,

*Have we been robbed?*


But the evidence was clear,

Clear to the opposite.

It was merely the way Tasnim saw things.


Different, with secrets lurking

In the shadows of the house.

Shadows Tasnim was going to delve into.


She opened the front door,

Felt the cool air flush against her face,

Felt the remnants of homely dust greet her.


The lights were off,

Though gaps in the curtains

Caused slices of illumination to cut every room.

Tasnim walked up the stairs,

Legs feeling weak,

Whilst Riyad followed her through.


Her mother's room

Was on the far side

Of the hallway.


The room with the most privacy,

Though close enough

For Tasnim and Riyad to rescue.


And Harun, of course.

That boy never ceased

To rush through


The hallway, from his room

To his grandmother's room.

Tasnim now faced the grey door,

A door that looked dead and buried,

As if resurrected from underneath.

The look was creepy, but Tasnim knew


That it was merely a trick of the light.

Merely the play of her eyes,

Making her imagine things that weren't real.


Her mother hadn't turned into a ghost

Doomed to haunt her room,

And Tasnim was only here for the truth,


And nothing but the truth.

Tasnim held the door handle

And felt a warmth rush through,


From her fingertips to her toes,

Zinging across nape and head.

Tasnim held her breath,

Glanced back at Riyad,

Who offered her a smile.

Then she turned and stepped inside.

# 55

The room was as Tasnim remembered

The day her mother had passed.

Tasnim made sure to clean it


Every day, or every other.

Her mother didn't make huge messes,

But Tasnim felt it necessary


To give the only mother in her life.

The premium treatment at home.

Riyad helped out, too,


Since he viewed her mother

As if his own,

Especially after they moved in together.

Her mother's bed held a green duvet,

With a red pillow, dark red,

As if symbolising Bangladesh.


The colours were spread evenly,

And the bed was made.

Tasnim remembered with a jolt—


She'd been the one to make it.

Tasnim glanced left,

And found the cabinet of jewellery—


It was from her mother's wedding,

From Tasnim's father who'd passed away.

He'd bought Tasnim's mother


Shiny necklaces and bracelets,

And even a watch thirty years before.

Tasnim's mother wished to pass it down,

Pass it down to her.

But Tasnim never accepted.

She loved jewellery,


But didn't wish to encroach on her mother's

Only physical memory

Of her own husband.


Perhaps if Tasnim's father was alive,

Then Tasnim would wear the jewellery with pride.

But now, she merely wrapped her scarf tight


And walked through the room's centre.

Her legs violently jittered,

As that familiar grief crept up on her.


The grief of losing her mother—

But not only that. Added was the grief

Of not knowing, fully, who it was she lost.

A double loss, truly.

As if her mother had died,

And with that death her memory.


Tasnim peered at the jewellery,

Then opened the wardrobe.

All her mother's clothes were there—


Old *salwar kameez*,

With sequins shimmering beneath

The silky and smooth fabric.


Tasnim had a similar few of her own,

That Harun particularly loved,

Since they were soft to touch,


And he ran his hands through them.

Tasnim pushed her hands through

The flurry of *salwar kameez*,

Until she reached the back,

Right in the corner,

Where there existed a little key.


She used that to open the cabinet

Stuffed with expensive jewellery,

Then searched through—


In search of what, she didn't know.

She looked at a watch,

Then at other pieces of gold and silver.


Perhaps there was a clue there

For her to decipher.

Perhaps her mother's secrets


Lay in a particular bracelet.

Or perhaps Tasnim was barking

Right up the wrong tree.

Riyad stood beside Tasnim,

Looking at a necklace himself.

"Here, I found something," he said.


But the moment was anticlimactic.

Since it was merely an inscription.

'From S.,' was all it read.


"That doesn't mean anything, does it?"

That was Tasnim's question,

And answers wouldn't be given.


"I don't know," Riyad said,

Placing the necklace back.

Tasnim sighed, closed the cabinet,


Grabbed the key,

And even though her mother was gone,

Placed it back in the wardrobe's corner.

But her hands brushed something else,

Something wedged on the other side.

Something she'd never believed to find.


Her mother's diary.

Something Tasnim hadn't seen

In over twenty years.


She had only one vague memory

Of her mother reading the diary,

Or writing in it at all.


Tasnim brought it out.

The cover was leather,

Hardbound, and heavy,


Like the secrets inside,

Were meant to be kept.

Tasnim clutched it to her chest.

The book had suffered neglect.

Since the edges were fraying,

Decomposing as if before death.


Tasnim knew the diary

Was where the secrets were kept.

But she couldn't read them here.


Tasnim didn't know what to think.

So she nodded to Riyad,

And they both quickly left.

# 56

Tasnim had been seven,

One of those kids that were

Always a little dishevelled.

Her mother had been in the garden

Of their council home,

With the peeling walls,

Broken shed,

And more weeds than spikes

In a hornet's nest.

And yet it had been Tasnim's home,

And she had loved it.

It was early morning,

Sunlight creeping in as if spying

On Tasnim's mother as she sat.

Tasnim slowly walked out,


Intending to surprise her mum.

"Boo," she'd shouted,

And her mother almost toppled over.


Giggles seized Tasnim,

And her mother looked

Less than amused, more bemused,


Though her eyes betrayed a smile.

And in her hands Tasnim had seen it—

The diary, leather-bound. Brand new.


"What's that?" Tasnim had asked,

But her mother snatched it back.

"Nothing, *bacha*," she'd said,

And that was the end of that.

For the next few years,

Tasnim had always wondered,


What her mother wrote in the journal,

But then the thought slipped from her mind,

And her thoughts went to more important things,


Like school and then marriage,

And then her son, Harun.

But all throughout the confusion,


Was her mother's diary

The real hidden key

To solving every mystery?

# 57

*Found something,*

Tasnim texted Hanna,

Whilst they were in the car.

They being Riyad and her,

Driving back to Aunt Jolly's house.

They had around a half hour

Left on the journey,

And Tasnim sat back,

With the diary in her bag,

Itching to get it open

And read what was inside.

But she had to bide her time.

Riyad spoke over the engine's rumble.

"You look happier," he said,

"Not that you *should*, given what happened.

But you look like you're coping."

Tasnim sighed,

Fingers jittering in her lap.

Was she coping, really?

Or merely using a coping mechanism

That would soon run out, shut down?

"You've been more supportive

Than anyone else I can imagine," Tasnim said.

She reached over, placed a cold hand against warm,

"I've put you through the ringer."

"That's fine," Riyad said with a laugh,

Eyes glued to the road,

"That's my job as a husband,

Whether I like it or not.

And I'm sure you'd do the same,


That's what marriage is about.

Helping each other get to Jannah."

At the mention of Jannah,


Tasnim quickly checked her phone.

"*Asr's* in about an hour," she said,

"Want to go to the mosque and pray?"


Riyad gave her such a wide smile

That it almost made all

Her troubles go away.

# 58

After *Asr*, and then *Maghrib*,

They all sat down to eat dinner.

Tasnim had helped Aunt Jolly


Cook an array of desi curries—

From spinach with jackfruit seeds

To chicken filled with too much spice,


But oh was it tasty!

Fruits were on the side,

In a bowl the size of London.


But Tasnim was burning inside,

With the need to head upstairs,

And pop open the diary

And check what her mother had to hide.

Check what the reality was.

When they'd first arrived


Back at Aunt Jolly's house,

Tasnim said she'd found something,

So she hadn't lied,


But she also said she'd tell

Aunt Jolly what it was

Once she'd gone through it herself.


But she hadn't done that yet,

And though the food was nice,

And warm, and filled her belly,


It didn't quench her thirst for knowledge.

Harun sat beside her, leg kicking

Against hers almost incessantly.

"I'm sorry," Tasnim said quietly.

Harun looked at her a little confused.

"Why sorry, *Amma*?"


"Because I haven't stayed with you

Whilst we've been here. And that's my fault."

Once upon a time, Tasnim would've brushed it away,


But she knew keeping kids in the dark—

That wasn't the way to move forward.

If her mother hadn't done that, then perhaps


Tasnim would be sitting now with an aunt

That she knew for over twenty years.

An aunt she loved for years.


And they would have a history together,

And share memories with each other,

And help each other through the grief.

But no, her mother's secrets had

Sliced all that into two, and Tasnim

Couldn't estrange Harun the same way.


"I'll tell you the truth," Tasnim said,

"The whole truth when I find it.

Do you trust me on that, my son?"


Harun looked more than confused,

But he merely gave an endearing smile,

Similar to his father's,


And wrapped Tasnim in a side hug.

The others at the table saw that,

And all chuckled at the sight.


And soon after dinner ended,

They'd all eaten,

And Isha would clock in

After about half an hour.

Tasnim asked Riyad,

For probably the hundredth time,


To occupy Harun with something.

Then Tasnim went upstairs,

Sat on her bed,


And delved into the diary,

To find the secrets of her mother.

Secrets to solve the mysteries.

# 59

The withered pages felt

Rough under Tasnim's skin,

As if mimicking her grief,


Like the diary somehow

Knew she wasn't its owner

Who was touching it,


But rather someone foreign,

Someone who wished to know its secrets,

Rather than placing more in.


Tasnim found nothing

Important to her mysteries

At the diary's beginning.

Her mother seemed to use

The diary to log her thoughts,

Log her feelings,


As some kind of therapy

Without paying for a psychologist.

She wrote things about Allah,


Wrote down her *duas*

For Tasnim to find love

When she grew older.


Tasnim read on,

Wondering what else she would uncover.

The voice in the back of her head,


That pesky voice of doubt,

Spoke out now,

Telling her to retreat,

To place the diary back,

And to not read further

For it could change her beliefs.


But Tasnim for once ignored that voice,

And turned the next page,

And then her eyes bulged


At what met her face.

*'My love Salman,*

*Know how I have missed you*


*More than you can imagine.*

*But I cannot speak to you,*

*For we are separated*


*By things I cannot control.*

*That wedding ring*

*Sits in my drawer,*

*But I cannot wear it for*

*It might make my daughter question*

*Reality, and I cannot let her know.'*


*Know what?* Tasnim's heart shouted,

Realising the 'S.' inscription meant Salman,

And her mind connected the dots.


Hajji wasn't his first name,

But the title of someone who'd done Hajj.

Rattled, intrigued, Tasnim then read on.


*'I have a little sister,*

*With whom I was separated at her birth.*

*She lived in foster care,*


*Due to my father's drunkenness,*

*And my mother sent her away,*

*For she could not deal with two alone.*

*I do not blame her, though it saddens me.*

*I know we are separated,*

*Salman, but I trust you with this.*


*I am writing this in my diary,*

*To get this off my chest.*

*But I will also enclose a letter,*


*For you to properly read.*

*I have a friend*

*Who is in the police.*


*She will get this letter to you*

*After I die, after my demise,*

*She will connect my daughter to you.*


*And if not, then to my sister.*

*I have already written letters for her*

*A long time ago,*

*Letters of needing support.*

*I need my daughter to have support,*

*From other than her mother,*

*Because support is needed in life.*

*My mother forced you to divorce me,*

*Made my life hell more than a drunken*

*Father ever could.*

*You know she never liked you,*

*Said your village was of low standing.*

*I know we never cared,*

*But I chose her wishes,*

*Steeped in the mindless parts of culture,*

*Instead of choosing my own.*

*It was the biggest mistake,*

*My beloved Salman,*

*To convince you to divorce me*

*At the wishes of my mother.*

*I hope you are enjoying life,*


*With your new wife*

*And your other children, if they exist.*

*At least, that way*


*I wish the best for you.*

*I'm sorry for not telling you*

*About your own daughter.*


*I fell pregnant not three weeks after*

*Our divorce, but my mother told me*

*Not to say, to lie to the government's face.*


*Again, another mistake,*

*But I was gullible at the time.*

*I hope my daughter avoids the same,*

*Because she deserves more in life.*

*That is all, Salman.*

*If you read this, then know*


*Soon you will be once again connected,*

*To your daughter, Tasnim Alam.*

*And I am truly sorry, even whilst in death.'*

# 60

Tasnim's hands shook
As she read the last of the letter.
Her eyes bulged,

And heat washed over her
In waves upon waves,
As if attempting to drown her.

But she was drowning
In her own thoughts,
In those seas that were wrought

With worries and problems,
And she felt that grief
Tumble across her again.

Grief for the father

She should've had,

But didn't due to stubbornness.


So Aunt Jolly had been adopted?

So when she inherited

From her grandfather,


She'd been talking of the family

She'd grown up in,

Not the parents she was born to.


Tasnim let the white of the duvet

Attack her as she sat on the bed.

She sat contemplating


How her life was a lie.

Her father had been alive

The entire time,

And yet for some reason,

Her mother hadn't connected them.

In Tasnim's mind,


The dots all connected.

She caught her mother many times

Staring at her with a solemn look


Painted in her eyes,

As if she was afraid of losing

Her only daughter to the truth.


Hence she would only tell Tasnim

After she died, so she was safe in her grave

Whilst Tasnim dealt with the after effects


Roaring through her life.

A knock on the door

Caused her thoughts to subside.

"You ready to go *Isha*?" Riyad asked,

Harun by his side, holding his hand.

Harun, Tasnim's own child

Who had a father,

Whilst she had none.

Or maybe she could find him again.

Tasnim, without another word,

Roared past Riyad and Harun,

In search of Aunt Jolly.

# 61

Aunt Jolly was in the kitchen

Making tea for her husband,

Making tea for Aadam.

"Auntie, what happened

To your friend Yasmin.

The one who wrote the article.

Does she know where Hajji Salman lives?"

Tasnim's eyes were wide, suspense driving

Her to storm over and stare her aunt in the face.

"Hajji Salman is my dad," Tasnim then said,

Unable to contain her excitement.

Despite the revelations in the last few minutes,

She'd gained a father

That she could visit and be close with.

One parent lost had caused another gained,


And though she had wished for both,

She was content with one at a time.

"I spoke to Yasmin," Aunt Jolly said,


Her gaze slipping to the ground,

And Tasnim felt the kitchen chill,

Despite the kettle blaring aloud.


"What did she say?" Tasnim asked.

"Hajji Salman passed away,

Three years ago.


I'm sorry, Tasnim,

I truly am."

And she engulfed Tasnim in an embrace.

# 62

Tasnim was in *Sidepark Cafe* again,

Staring out at the children play.

With those children were Riyad

And his son, Harun.

They were on the swings now,

Harun wishing to go higher,

But Riyad usually played it safe,

And didn't push him as hard.

Tasnim smiled as she watched,

Felt glasses clink behind her

As other customers grabbed their orders.

Tasnim nursed her own coffee.

She didn't need the caffeine,

Only the taste.

Something sweet after the bitterness.


Hanna had been surprised to learn

The truth of Tasnim's life.

But as always, and perhaps she


Was the only friend like this,

Hanna was supportive,

And would be there when Tasnim returned.


The door then opened,

Causing a small jingle.

This customer wore a blue scarf


Mimicking the freshness of the sky above.

She walked over to Tasnim,

Sat down beside her

And then took off her bag.

It was Aisha, a former police officer,

And a revert to Islam.


The one who had kept her mother's secrets,

And kept them all along.

Tasnim said *salaam*,


And then cut to the chase.

She didn't have time to waste,

Since she wished to be out there with her son.


"Why didn't you tell the truth?"

That was what Tasnim asked.

"Didn't you read the letter she wrote?"


Tasnim shook her head at Aisha's reply.

"Do you know how hard it is

Growing up without a father?

Without the second part,

Always feeling like I'm less than others,

For something I didn't ask?"


"I can't imagine," Aisha said,

"But the truth is, your mother told me,

If your father already passed,


That I should connect you with your aunt,

And leave his existence a secret.

She didn't want to bathe yourself


In some kind of double grief.

Trust me, that's the worst thing you want."

Tasnim shook her head more violently.


"The truth is what's important.

Truth leads to truth,

Whereas lies only create more.

If you'd told me the truth,

I wouldn't have had to search.

This...anticipating wouldn't be in my heart."


"You are at peace now?" Aisha asked,

"Or do you still grieve?

You do not seem to me


To be grief-ridden.

Unless you hide it well."

Tasnim didn't say anything more.


Her grief was a confusing thing.

Threatening to break her, but also being unable to.

As if Tasnim had defences now


That came to the rescue.

"I'll see you some other time,"

Tasnim said, then gave *salaam*.

She walked out of *Sidepark Cafe*,

Into the sunshine,

And let the truth grace her face.

# 63

Tasnim stood outside

The wall of brick,

Grey and brown

Chafed raw by the wind

Over years and years and years.

The bricks of the cemetery.

"Are you sure you want to go inside?"

That was what Riyad asked.

It was the cemetery housing Hajji Salman.

Tasnim looked at the gate,

Arched like an Arabian palace.

Her heart was split in two ways—

To go in or stay out.

And Tasnim chose the one she felt

Was right, was the truth of herself.


She chose to remain out.

Harun was with Riyad,

And gave Tasnim a hug.


"I love you *Amma*," he said,

"Even *more* than yesterday."

Tasnim smiled, repeated the same.


And it was the truth,

Not a mother's lie,

Not a lifelong secret.


Riyad offered her a smile,

Then took their son inside

To see the grave of his grandfather.

But Tasnim didn't need to go.

She already had the family,

The one Allah had given her,


And that family was enough for her.

She could always be chasing the past,

Chasing what she had lost.


But grief was only meant to be

A lamenting of what was gone—

Not a chasing after it


Like she could rewind time

And bring those people back again.

Tasnim let the breeze course over her,


And despite the setting,

The sun's light beamed across her face,

Washing her with its radiance.

Despite the secrets,

Tasnim had found the truth

Of her mother and father.


But she'd found bigger truths,

More important truths—

The truth of her current family,


That being the best mother, wife, friend, niece,

Was better than chasing

After ghosts that didn't exist.


And the truth that Allah

Was the One who gave blessings,

Was the One who took life


And who gave life,

Was the One who imbued

The world with truth.

And He had led Tasnim to that truth—

The truth of Himself, most of all.

And Tasnim, despite all the falsehoods


That may try to break her,

Would latch onto that greater truth,

And hold on till she met her Maker.

# Newsletter

For writing updates and info on new releases, sign up to our newsletter!

# About S. H. Miah

S. H. Miah is the founder of Muslim Fiction Project. An initiative to produce high-quality Muslim fiction. Written for Muslims. By a Muslim.

When not writing, S. H. Miah enjoys spending time with family and friends, charging through his own reading list, and of course having a bit too large an obsession with spiral-bound notebooks.

For more information about Muslim Fiction Project, please visit: https://www.muslimfictionproject.com

# About MFP

The Muslim Fiction Project, MFP, is an initiative started by S. H. Miah to publish works of fiction that promote Islamic messages for Muslims all around the world.

Written for Muslims. By a Muslim.

Visit our website to see what other stories you could sink your teeth into!

Milton Keynes UK
Ingram Content Group UK Ltd.
UKHW010652250923
429338UK00001B/47